Hi Blue Sky

"My friend, My best friend"

I value you like gold
Warmth to my cold

Laughter to my frown
Playtime is harmony, our joy is sky-bound

Forever young we'll grow old
You are the greatest truth ever told

We travel along time like free-flowing wind
Your journey is mine, because you are my friend.

Hi Blue Sky, Hey Kind Wind,
Can you give a message to Tay, my best friend?

Tell him I love his doll and I'll never give it away
Tell him that it's Keke and I have something to say:

Please make sure that he eats his favorite lunch;
Bananas, rice, and sweet chicken with a delicious crunch.
Tell him that I miss our sports and I miss our pranks.

Oh, and when you see him,
can you also give him my thanks?

He did hate to lose, especially when we would race,
Tell him I'll stop laughing when he makes his angry face.

I miss our jokes, I miss our fun,
I miss our adventures under the sun.
I want to know if he has happy thoughts of me,
or if he simply has none.

I do not know if he was sick, if he was tired,
or if he just wanted to leave.

Tell him when he comes back,
I promise to stop blowing my nose on his sleeve.

When he comes back, we will play everywhere.
The moon, the sun, the rivers and all the tall trees.

Blue Sky, Kind Wind,
Can you make sure he gets this doll I made for him?

Please?

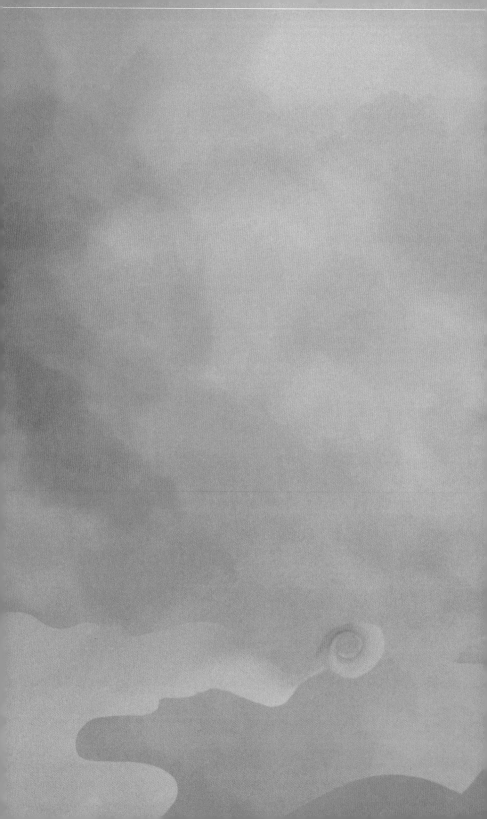

Jeffrey L. Cheatham II's passion for storytelling was evident from his days as a student at Seattle's John Muir Elementary School, where every written assignment he submitted was in the form of a story or comic. From that point on, he has been a passionate and ardent supporter of all things literary, even going so far as to writing two children's books "The Family Jones and The Eggs of Rex" and the award-winning "Why is Jane so Mad?"

Date:_____/_____/_____

Dear friend,

_____
_____
_____
_____
_____
_____
_____
_____
_____
_____
_____
_____
_____
_____
_____
_____
_____
_____
_____
_____
_____
_____
_____
_____
_____
_____
_____
_____

Sincerely, _____

Thank you so Much!
Let Creativity drive your heart!
Enjoy!

Made in the USA
Columbia, SC
02 June 2019